Angelina and the Princess

For Tara and Alexandra   KH

To Mary Craig, with love   HC

PUFFIN BOOKS

Penguin Books Ltd, Registered Offices: 80 Strand, London WC2R 0RL, England

First published by Aurum Press Ltd 1984
Published by Viking and in Puffin Books 2001
This edition published in Puffin Books 2002
3 5 7 9 10 8 6 4

Printed in Italy

ISBN 0–140–56916–2

Angelina
and the Princess

Story by **Katharine Holabird** Illustrations by **Helen Craig**

Angelina was much too excited to sleep. The students at Miss Lilly's Ballet School had been asked to dance for Her Royal Highness, The Princess of Mouseland. Mr Lightfoot, Director of the famous Royal Ballet Company, was coming tomorrow to help Miss Lilly choose the best ballerinas for the special performance. Angelina wanted a leading part so much that she worked on her pliés and pirouettes far into the night when she should have been sound asleep.

The next morning Angelina woke up feeling terrible.
Her head ached and her ears buzzed. Angelina's mother
took her temperature and shook her head sadly. "I'm
afraid you'll have to stay in bed," she said. "You can't
go to ballet school when you're not well."

But Angelina was determined to go. While her mother was busy downstairs Angelina packed her ballet bag …

… and tiptoed out of the house.

Angelina arrived at Miss Lilly's Ballet School just in time to join her friends Flora and Felicity and all the other ballerinas who were waiting to go on stage. Flora did a nimble leap and a delicate spin …

… and then it was Angelina's turn to dance. Her heart started beating like a drum and she couldn't remember what she was supposed to be doing.

The music started and Angelina knew she had to begin. She tried one step, she tried another …

… then she began twirling and spinning like a top until she was so dizzy she lost her balance, tripped on her pink ribbons, and tumbled down with a thump.

Flora and Felicity were given the leading roles in the Dance of the Flower Fairies. Later, Miss Lilly called for Angelina. "I'm afraid you will have to take a smaller part this time," she said, trying to be kind.

When Angelina got home her mother was very upset.
"How could you run away like that when I told you to
stay in bed?" she asked.

Angelina burst into tears. "I had to go to Miss Lilly's, but everything went wrong. I danced so badly for Mr Lightfoot, I will never be a real ballerina. I am not going to ballet school any more."

Angelina's mother hugged her and kissed her and
carried her upstairs, and in just a minute she was
fast asleep in her own bed again.

The next day Angelina's headache was gone.
She felt better, but she was still very sad.
"It's not fair!" said Angelina.

"Maybe not," her mother said gently, "but things don't always go our way. You can still do your best with whatever part you are given, and that will help the whole performance."

Angelina thought about what her mother had said. Then she returned to Miss Lilly's after all, and rehearsed very hard with the other ballerinas for the Royal Performance.

After she had learned her own part, she memorized
the Dance of the Flower Fairies while watching
Flora and Felicity.

On the day of the Royal Performance, just as the show
was about to begin, Flora tripped and sprained her ankle.
Everyone was terribly upset.

Mr Lightfoot and Miss Lilly turned to each other in
horror. "Who can do the part?" they cried. Angelina
was worried about Flora, but Susie stepped forward
and said, "Angelina can!"

Angelina showed Miss Lilly that she had learned the
dance by heart. "But what about Flora?" she asked.

"Don't worry," said Miss Lilly, "we have a treat for
her …"

… So Flora was happy because she was invited to sit right next to The Princess of Mouseland. Mr Lightfoot and Miss Lilly were happy because the performance could go on. Angelina was happy because she did the Dance of the Flower Fairies without forgetting a single step. The Princess of Mouseland was happy because she loved ballet.

When the performance was over she congratulated Angelina and thanked her warmly for saving the show.